BUSTER

and the

Pet Detectives

Janeen Brian

Illustrated by Bettina Guthridge

SuPa
DOOPERS

sundance
A Haights Cross Communications Company

Published by
Sundance Publishing
P.O. Box 1326
234 Taylor Street
Littleton, MA 01460
800-343-8204
www.sundancepub.com

Project commissioned and managed by
Lorraine Bambrough-Kelly, The Writer's Style
Designed by Cath Lindsey/design rescue

First published 1999 by
Addison Wesley Longman Australia Pty Limited
95 Coventry Street
South Melbourne 3205 Australia
Exclusive United States Distribution: Sundance Publishing

ISBN 0-7608-6636-8

Printed in Canada

Contents

Chapter 1

Going to Be Rich

"Hey, Mack!" cried Janey from the living room. "Our first job!" She slammed down the telephone and leaped in the air.

Mack, her twin brother, hurtled from the bedroom.

"Who?" he cried.

"A Mrs. Maxwell." Then Janey giggled, "She's got a poodle called Smumble."

"Smumble-bumble!" shrieked Mack. When he stopped laughing, he asked, "So, Janey, when do we walk Smumble?"

"Mondays, Wednesdays, and Fridays, right after school," his sister said.

"We'll be rich!" cried Mack. "I can save for my dirt bike."

"And I can take tae kwon do lessons!" said Janey. "Come on—let's find Buster and tell him the good news!"

Chapter 2

Dog Walkers

Buster was the twins' ancient dog. He looked up at them through a shock of brown hair and blinked at the news.

"Great to see you're so excited, Buster!" grinned Mack. He gave the old dog a scratch on his head.

"Now, Mack, he's not a puppy anymore," remarked Janey protectively. She hated to think of Buster growing old. Then she added, "I wonder what Smumble's like."

They found out Monday afternoon. Mrs. Maxwell lived in an enormous house. It was covered in ivy and set at the end of a very long driveway.

"Oh," said the woman, eyeing the twins up and down. "You sounded older on the phone."

"We've had a great deal of experience," said Janey, sounding creamily sincere. Mack held out the card they'd printed on the computer.

> DOG WALKERS Have your dog lovingly exercised by two fit dog-lovers.
> Reasonable rates.
> Phone Mack and Janey, 555–1221.

"Very well," nodded the woman through a haze of perfume. "Here's Smumble." And she handed over a large pom-pom on legs. There were pink bows and pink booties laced around the pom-pom's ankles.

"Take this, too," added Mrs. Maxwell. She handed over a plastic bag that had fringe all around it. "I keep Smumble's special doggy treats in this pouch," she said. "I just know that my itsy-bitsy doggy-woggy will behave *perfectly* for you, so you can use these to reward her."

With straight faces, Janey and Mack told Mrs. Maxwell that they felt lucky to be walking such a perfect doggy-woggy!

But when they reached the bus stop at the end of the road, Smumble sat down and refused to go any farther.

"Come on, Smumble," pleaded Mack, frowning. "Janey, what are we going to do? We can't drag her along like a pull toy!"

"We'll have to carry her," said Janey.

"Perfect doggy-woggy, my foot!" said Mack. "Next time we'll bring Buster. He can show her how a good dog behaves!"

Chapter 3

Go, Buster!

On Wednesday, they turned up at the house with Buster on a leash. Mrs. Maxwell's top lip curled upward.

"I thought you only walked the *best* dogs,"
she said, peering down her nose at Buster.

"Oh," explained Janey with a smile, "we'll
keep them *completely* separate."

"Mmm," murmured Mrs. Maxwell. She handed over Smumble, who was wearing a little polka-dot jacket. Today she had yellow ribbons tied onto her neck and tail and front legs.

At the bus stop, Smumble repeated her sit-down act. Mack clenched his teeth. Janey sighed. But Buster walked up behind Smumble and, with one swift nudge of his nose, gave her a gentle push. To the twins' astonishment, the little fluff-ball got to her feet and trotted on.

"Way to go, Buster!" cried Mack. The old dog lifted his chin with pride.

Chapter 4

Pet Detectives

The next time Janey and Mack went to Mrs. Maxwell's house, she was *very* upset.

"She's gone! My baby is gone!" sobbed Mrs. Maxwell, holding her forehead.

The twins looked at each other in surprise. Did Mrs. Maxwell have a *baby?*

"I'd just finished dressing her in her pale blue outfit. Oh, how she loves that outfit!" wept Mrs. Maxwell. "And, well, the gate must have been open because she's gone!"

"Ah! Now I see! Your baby is *Smumble*. It's Smumble who is gone!" said Janey.

"I've looked in the house, the garden, the stables, the garage, and even the pool!" Mrs. Maxwell's hand flew to her mouth in horror at the thought of what she might have found there.

Mack gave Janey a nudge and a nod. Then he said, "Well, it's a good thing that we're here now!"

Mrs. Maxwell snorted. "I don't see why you would say that. In fact, young man, I think that is a rather heartless comment. After all, Smumble is not here."

"Ah," said Mack, "but walking dogs is only *one* part of our business."

Janey gave him a questioning look.

"Because," continued Mack, "we're also Pet Detectives!"

Janey's eyes snapped wide open.

"Don't you worry about Smumble, Mrs. Maxwell. If anyone can find her for you, it's us—right, Janey?"

Janey nodded dumbly.

"There'll be a reward, of course," said
Mrs. Maxwell. She covered her eyes and
reached for her handkerchief.

On the way back down the driveway, Janey shook her head. "Why did you say we'd find Smumble? How are we going to do that? She could be anywhere!"

Mack replied, "Don't you see, Janey? That dog couldn't have gone too far. Before we brought Buster with us the other day, that dressed-up floor mop wouldn't go any farther than the bus stop."

Chapter 5

No Way!

Janey and Mack got busy on the computer. They printed out a bunch of leaflets to give to people. They placed an ad in the local paper. And they handed out posters for shopkeepers to put in their windows.

At the end of the afternoon, Mack put his feet up on his desk. He said confidently, "Now, we wait."

And wait they did. During the next few days, there were no phone calls about Smumble. There was no news at all!

"Some Pet Detectives we are," groaned Janey, leaning against the trunk where they kept their old clothes and costumes. She worriedly twisted long strands of her hair. "What do we do now?"

Mack only frowned.

"You can't think of anything else, can you?" said Janey.

Suddenly an idea popped into Janey's head. "Mack!" she said excitedly.

Kneeling quickly on the floor, she began searching through the trunk. When she found the costume she was looking for, a smile spread across her face.

Janey had been a sheep in a school play last year. She turned toward Mack and held up the costume she had worn.

"We can dye the wool a cream color and comb it to make it look more shaggy," she announced. "Then *you* can be Smumble!"

"No way!" cried Mack. "I won't do it!"

31

Chapter 6

Honey Territory

At the shopping center, Mack whispered, "I feel like an idiot. Why do I have to do this? Why not you?"

"Because I thought of it," replied Janey smugly. She straightened the sign on Mack's chest. It read HAVE YOU SEEN THIS DOG?

"Stop fidgeting," Janey ordered, as they stood in front of the juice bar next to the HUMBLE HONEY counter.

"I'll get you for this, Janey Thompson!" muttered Mack, spluttering wool from his mouth.

A few people asked what they were doing. Then a big, furry brown bear approached them. The words HUMBLE HONEY BEAR were written on his hat, and there was no question about his mood.

"Clear out!" a deep voice muttered through a slit in its mouth. "I don't want any competition. This is honey territory!"

Chapter 7

On the Trail?

"Now what?" asked Janey later that night. "Come on, Mack! *You* said we were Pet Detectives. It's your turn for an idea."

"Well, you know those ribbons . . ." he began.

"What ribbons?" Janey asked.

"The yellow ones Smumble was wearing the last time we walked her."

"What about them?" said Janey curiously.

"See, the one around her tail was loose, so I took it off to keep it from getting lost."

"Yes," said Janey, trying to follow her brother's train of thought.

"I found it in my pocket earlier today. I guess I must have forgotten to tie it back on Smumble's tail."

"Great work, sherlock," sighed Janey. "We have a ribbon. All we need now is the dog to go with it!"

"I know, I know," said Mack. "But that's where Buster comes in."

And he waited until Janey slowly opened her mouth and cried, "Got it!"

Crouching down and patting the old dog, Janey spoke softly to him. "Buster, Mack and I have a problem. Do you remember that silly Smumble? Well, she's gone and gotten herself lost, and we're supposed to find her for Mrs. Maxwell. We've tried everything, but no luck . . . so we were hoping that *you* could help us."

Janey gave Buster a good long sniff of the ribbon Mack had discovered in his pocket. Then she said, "OK, Buster. It's up to you, now. Go find Smumble!"

Mack held Buster's leash and allowed him to follow his nose. Every so often, Janey placed the ribbon in front of his face to give him another sniff of Smumble's scent. Then she'd give him a special dog biscuit for encouragement.

Buster walked along, sniffing here and there. He seemed to be having a fine time. When they came to the bus stop, Buster halted.

"Could be something," cried Mack, looking hopeful.

But the old dog only sniffed the two people sitting on the bench at the bus stop. Buster wagged his tail when the little girl started to pat him. Then her mother told her to sit down and leave the strange dog alone.

Buster walked on. He looked as though he was enjoying himself. He poked his nose into all sorts of interesting places. But after they'd searched the park and the downtown area, Janey said, "I don't know, Mack. I don't think that Smumble would ever have come this far on her own."

Mack sighed. "Let's go a bit farther. Buster seems to be on the trail. Give him another whiff of Smumble's ribbon."

On they walked, past the gas station, the church, and a long stretch of open field. And after that, they started down the road that went past the junkyard.

Buster kept tugging on his leash.

"This is crazy," Janey groaned. "We'll be in the next county soon! We should head back right now."

"Let's keep going for just a little bit longer," Mack replied.

Chapter 8

What a Nose!

The junkyard was almost colorful. Parts and pieces of junk were scattered about. Other junk lay in a big jumble.

"I'm not going in there," said Janey.

However, Buster had other ideas. He pulled sharply on his leash, and it shot out of Mack's hand.

Chasing Buster into the junkyard, Janey shouted, "He's only after food. He thinks he'll find something to eat in there!"

But when Buster reached a large, rusty piece of metal shaped like a water tank, he came to a halt. He barked loudly and wagged his tail furiously.

A whiskered face shot out from behind the metal. It belonged to Mr. Donner, the man in charge of the junkyard.

Mr. Donner stepped forward carrying a basket and a bundle of things under his arm. "Hi, Janey and Mack! What a nice surprise!" His eyes twinkled.

"Hello, Mr. Donner" replied the twins.

Janey knew that Mr. Donner would like them to stay and talk, but she also knew they'd already been gone too long. "We'd like to visit with you, Mr. Donner, but we've got to head home," she explained.

"Nice dog," said Mr. Donner, bending his head toward Buster. Gently, he stretched out one hand, and to the twins' surprise, Buster stepped up and licked it.

Smiling at Janey and Mack, Mr. Donner continued, "He's been specially loved. I can always tell."

It was then that Janey's nose wrinkled.
There was a strong smell of fish. Where was
the odor coming from? She turned toward
Mack, but he was staring curiously at the
piles of stuff that lay all around. Trust
Mack—his room was always filled with
junk!

"I run this junkyard, but I'm also a magpie," Mr. Donner explained with a grin. "You know—a collector." Mack felt his cheeks grow warm, but Mr. Donner added, "Don't be embarrassed, Mack. I just saw you looking at my things. Most people call it junk. I don't. I collect stuff, and then I make new things out of old."

Janey knew her brother was itching to see what Mr. Donner had gathered. But she said firmly, "Come on, Mack. Let's go."

Mack sighed. "Oh, all right," he said.

Suddenly there was a bark. Buster's ears pricked up. Mack and Janey glanced at each other quickly. If it wasn't Buster barking, who was it?

Mr. Donner reached gently through a hole in the tank and said, "This is something I didn't set out to collect. But I don't know what to do with her. Her dog tag is gone, so I can't get in touch with her owner. I don't know who she belongs to or where she lives."

When he held up the dog, Mack and Janey
gasped. They stared openmouthed at the
dog, then at Mr. Donner, then at the dog
again.

"It's her, isn't it?" Mack whispered through
tight lips.

"It's her," nodded Janey in disbelief.

Smumble's fur was smudged and untidy,
but it was definitely her!

"How did you . . . where was she?" asked Janey. She cautiously stretched her hand toward Smumble.

"She was here," said Mr. Donner, pointing around the junkyard. "I found her several days ago. She seemed very tired."

"I'm not surprised," said Mack. "She's usually a wimp when it comes to walking any distance."

"Oh?" said Mr. Donner.

"We've just started taking her for walks," said Janey. "I don't think she'd done much walking before we came along."

"I see," said Mr. Donner, stroking Smumble's none-too-clean fur.

"But it's good you know her. You'll be able to take her home." He gave Janey a long, knowing look. "She's a lovely little thing, but I think she's been overprotected—you know, treated like a baby." Janey glanced up at Mr. Donner. "I guess she just took off," he went on. "She was after an adventure, that's all. Just like we humans are!"

Janey laughed. Wasn't that exactly what Mack and she were doing?

"She was hungry," Mr. Donner went on. "I didn't have any dog food, but I did have a couple of cans of sardines. I opened them and gave her those. Boy, did she gobble them up!"

Ah, thought Janey . . . that explains the fishy smell!

"Well, thanks," said Mack with a big grin on his face.

Janey thought, I know Mack. He's thinking about the reward.

"I'm glad she's not hurt," her brother added. He held out his arms for Smumble. "Here, I'll carry her home."

"Mack, maybe there's hope for you yet," Janey laughed. Turning to Mr. Donner, she waved. Then she said, "Come on, Buster. You get a special treat for dinner tonight. What a detective's nose you've got!"

Chapter 9

Sardines, of All Things

"Smumble!" cried Mrs. Maxwell, her eyes gleaming. "My darling! Oh, where have you been, my little tootsy-wootsy?"

"She's safe," said Janey. There were some adults who wouldn't understand about kids or dogs wanting adventures. Mrs. Maxwell was *definitely* one of them!

The following day, when Janey and Mack turned up with Buster to take Smumble for a walk, Mrs. Maxwell had a couple of surprises for them. One was a check—their reward for finding Smumble.

The second was another job.

"My dear, dear friend Mr. Franklin has a beagle, Romley. He thinks you'd be just perfect to take charge of his precious pet."

"Great," said Janey, writing down the man's phone number.

"And something else," said Mrs. Maxwell. "It's a funny thing, but since you brought Smumble back home, she won't touch her gourmet food."

"Oh?" said Mack.

"Yes, it's strange," said Mrs. Maxwell, with just the faintest upturning of her nose. "She's taken an extraordinary liking to sardines! Imagine—*sardines*, of all things!"

About the Author
Janeen Brian

Janeen learned to love words and reading when she was a very young child. By the time she was eight years old, she had already decided to become a teacher.

As an adult, Janeen became a teacher-librarian and the mother of two daughters, and she began writing. Janeen has done all kinds of writing—books, poetry and verse, fiction and nonfiction, plays and scripts, and stories, poems, and plays for children's magazines. She also has acted with a professional children's theater group and has done dozens of television commercials and narration for videos.

Janeen owns a border collie named Nell. She lives in a seaside city in South Australia, not far from where she grew up.

About the Illustrator
Bettina Guthridge

Bettina Guthridge grew up in Australia. After studying art and teaching for three years, she moved to Italy with her husband. Ten years and two children later, Bettina and her family returned to Australia where she began illustrating children's books.

Bettina has illustrated many books for children—books written by well-known children's authors such as Ogden Nash and Roald Dahl. Her first picture book, *Matilda and the Dragon,* was followed by *Hurry Up Oscar.*

Bettina has had two successful exhibitions of sculptures made from objects she found on the beach. Her special pet is a border collie named Tex.